Druid's Quest

Story by Mark
Pictures by Zee

Matador
9 Priory Business Park,
Wistow Road, Kibworth Beauchamp,
Leicestershire. LE8 0RX
Tel: 0116 279 2299
Email: books@troubador.co.uk
Web: www.troubador.co.uk/matador
Twitter: @matadorbooks

ISBN 978 1788037 235

British Library Cataloguing in Publication Data.
A catalogue record for this book is available from the British Library.

Printed and bound by CPI Group (UK) Ltd, Croydon, CR0 4YY
Typeset in 16pt Century Gothic by Troubador Publishing Ltd, Leicester, UK

Matador is an imprint of Troubador Publishing Ltd

JF

Many thanks to Ro, Lynne, Jo, Katie and, especially, to Zee.

CHAPTER
ONE

Somewhere in the dark mountains of North Wales, deep within a remote hidden cave, lived a dragon. He was small and red and Welsh. His name was Druid.

Dragons had lived in these mountains for thousands of years, spending their time burning villages and stealing treasure. Long before the Romans came to the shores of Britain carrying their Golden Eagles, the dragons had collected treasures. In truth, they stole them. Dragons stole from anyone and anything. They would even steal from each other. A dragon's desire for treasure knew no bounds.

Druid was the last red dragon of Mynydd Mawr. All the other dragons were as green as grass. True to their colour, these dragons were of an envious nature. Out of jealousy and spite they had stolen Druid's treasure.

All dragons love gold.

GOLD!

That ancient precious metal. A dragon's deepest, most treacherous love. It was said that dragons could smell gold from miles away. It is gold that gives dragons the power to become mighty in size and magic. For without gold, a dragon cannot grow. What a dragon would not do even for the tiniest, inci-winciest speck of gold.

Terrorise whole countries!

Burn whole villages!

Eat whole families!

Today, dragons are rarely seen. After hundreds of years of plundering, they have all got so much treasure that they have grown fat and lazy.

They spend all their time deep within their carefully concealed, ancestral caves on Mynydd Mawr, sprawled on top of heaps of treasure, counting it over and over again, in order to estimate its present market value.

Stealing Druid's treasure was easy. They had simply waited until the small red dragon was out searching for more treasure to add to his tiny hoard, then the green dragons divided it between them. When Druid discovered that his small treasure had been stolen, he went to visit all the green dragons and asked each of them:

"Have you seen any of my treasure?"

The enormous green dragons had all gazed down from the top of their piles of gold, silver and jewels, and lied.

Some innocently.

Some outrageously.

Some until they were blue in the face.

All of them lied to their back teeth, and for a dragon that is a lot of teeth.

Druid knew they were lying, but there was nothing he could do. If he was not to remain small and hardly able to breathe fire forever, Druid had to find himself another treasure. Sitting at the entrance to his cave as the dawn rays reached him, he knew what he was going to do.

"I must go on a quest. A quest to find the greatest treasure in the world."

"The first places to search," thought Druid, "are castles."

Druid was not a good flyer. His wings were not very big and he soon became tired. He had not travelled very far before stopping to rest on the top of a great old stone castle. Harlech Castle was very old and so was the scent of the gold, which had been kept there hundreds of years before.

"Perhaps, none of the castles have treasures anymore," Druid sighed.

Druid's thoughts were interrupted by the sound of two men carrying a ladder up the stone steps below him.

"I don't care what anybody says, this is a long climb," puffed the man carrying the front end of the ladder. The second man grunted his agreement, trying to catch his breath. They put the ladder down and sat beside it. Druid peered down at them as they poured tea from their flasks.

"I hear David Evans's son has gone to work in London," remarked the first man. His companion slurped his tea and nodded.

"They say the streets of London are paved with gold…"

Neither man noticed the excited hiccup of smoke above them, nor the small glint of red pass over their heads and disappear into the distance.

The flight to London was long, but Druid's quest drove him.

CHAPTER TWO

The City of London was cold, grey and full of people. Druid was hungry, wet and tired. Darkness was creeping its way into the city. One by one the street lamps were flickering on. Druid's wings ached. He had found no streets paved with gold. He needed a rest. He landed heavily on a window sill and pressed against the glass. The window moved and the dragon lurched forward. Druid lay face down with his mouth full of feathers. Druid coughed the feathers away and crawled deeper into the bed.

Druid awoke at exactly the same time as the small boy lying next to him. They both blinked, gasped, screamed and fled. Druid's head hit the ceiling at speed. The boy dashed out of the room. The dragon lay dazed. The bedroom door edged open and a girl's face appeared cautiously behind it. The boy's face joined hers. Their eyes and mouths wide open.

"I told you. I told you it was a…" squeaked the boy.

"Sssh!" ordered the little dark haired girl, as they moved nearer the bed. Druid sat up. The children froze.

"What are you? I mean, who are you?" stammered the girl, remembering her manners. Druid stared back at her. The way she spoke was new to him, but like all dragons he had a gift for languages.

"Salutations. I am Druid. And you?" Druid bowed as he spoke the words slowly.

"What's a Druid?" challenged the boy.

"A dragon," came the proud reply.

"I'm Lucy, and this is my brother, Ben," announced the girl stepping nearer.

Druid stood to his full height to accept Lucy's hand.

"You're shorter than I am," declared Ben, as he and the dragon shook hands.

Large tears began to well up in Druid's eyes.

"Don't cry," pleaded Lucy, "he didn't mean to be nasty, did you, Ben?"

Lucy glared at her brother.

"No, I didn't," said Ben, trying to calm the dragon, "lots of my class are smaller than me."

The dragon was obviously hurt and more tears rolled down his scales.

"Please, don't cry," said Lucy.

"You might rust," added Ben.

"Ben!" exclaimed Lucy, turning on her brother. Ben tried to make up for his earlier blunders.

"Don't be upset, you'll get bigger when you get older."

This did not ease the dragon's misery. Lucy sternly put her finger to her lips to tell Ben that he had said enough. Ben shrugged and shut up. Slowly, with Lucy's coaxing, Druid's tears subsided. In a sad voice, water-logged with tears, Druid told them of his lost treasure, how he would never grow up and his new quest. Lucy and Ben sat on the bed listening to Druid's tale.

"Wow," from Ben. Lucy said nothing.

"Lucy! Benjamin! Come on, your breakfast's ready," came a voice far beyond the bedroom. "Hurry up or you'll be late for school!"

"We're late," gasped Ben, leaping off the bed for his clothes.

Lucy stopped at the bedroom door.

"Don't worry, Druid, we'll help you find the greatest treasure in the world," Lucy paused, "but only after school."

Druid and Ben stared after her.

That night, after tea, Lucy, Ben and Druid held a council of war.

As Druid and Ben munched through some peanut butter sandwiches, Lucy outlined her plan.

"Banks," reasoned Lucy, "have lots of money, so they must have some treasure. The bigger the bank, the more treasure inside it."

Lucy paused to make sure the other two understood.

Druid and Ben nodded.

"The biggest bank in London is the Bank of England," announced Lucy.

"How do you know?" interrupted Ben.

"Anna told me," answered Lucy. Ben accepted that.

"Anna's our sister, she's thirteen," he explained to Druid, who was busy licking his talons clean of peanut butter.

"This," continued Lucy, importantly, "is my plan."

CHAPTER THREE

Lucy strolled into the Bank of England. In her hand she held a bag containing her and Ben's savings. Ben followed more hesitantly, hauling another bag. In his bag, Druid was crammed. Lucy marched across the wide marble floor. Ben glanced nervously at the large old clock. It was 3.25pm. Five minutes until closing time. Lucy joined the queue for the cashier. Ben, struggling to carry Druid, tried to walk as calmly as he could to the heavy metal door, which led into the heart of the Bank of England.

"I wish to open an account," proclaimed Lucy. The cashier strained forward in her seat.

"Here is my money," Lucy went on, offering the cashier her small bag of assorted coins. The cashier shook her head slowly.

"I'm afraid, you're too young to open an account here, dear," replied the cashier, who had to sit almost on the desk to see the determined dark haired girl.

Lucy considered the cashier for a moment from beneath her fringe.

"In that case, I would like to see the Manager," demanded Lucy, in a tone which she had heard her mum use once in a supermarket.

"I'm afraid that won't be possible, dear. The Manager is a very busy man..." The cashier was not allowed to finish. Lucy stamped her foot.

"I want to see the Manager!"

Everybody in the bank was now looking at her and the cashier.

"Go on," called a voice from another queue, "let her see the Manager."

"I'd like to see him, too," shouted a different voice.

The cashier began to change colour.

"Why can't the girl see the Manager?" Everybody was joining in.

All the customers were now gathered around one till. Lucy slowly backed away from the crowd. Through the glass on the counter she saw a tall well-dressed gentleman come out of an arched oak and iron door.

The crowd was getting louder and ruder. Lucy joined her brother, just as the curved wood and metal door opened and the Manager strode out to see what all the noise was about. As the door swung silently shut behind the Manager, Lucy dashed through it, pulling Ben and bag after her.

As planned, they both scurried under the nearest two desks. Then they waited. Peeking up from her hiding place, Lucy saw the Manager return, wiping his brow with a starched white handkerchief.

Lucy's instructions had been to wait until all the lights had gone out, but Ben could not wait. He was getting pins and needles in both feet. He listened to the last few muffled 'good nights' from the bank staff, then stood up.

The lights went out as he did so, and the door closed behind the last member of staff. Ben bent down and opened his bag.

Druid squeezed out, flicking the creases out of his wings.

"Ben?" whispered Lucy.

"Over here," replied Ben.

"Over here," added Druid.

Lucy crawled from under her desk to join them.

"Where now, Luce?" asked Ben.

"Where now, Luce?" echoed Druid.

Ben took a slow suspicious look at the dragon. Lucy led the way to the double door and pushed through it into a long, dimly-lit corridor. The three conspirators crept along the passageway. Lucy stopped to read the name on each door.

"A C Q U I S I T I O N S," she read carefully.

"Who?" Ben asked.

Lucy ignored him. Druid flew on ahead of them, hovering a couple of feet above the ground. The corridor went off to both the left and right. Ben began to go left.

"Hold on," commanded Lucy, grabbing his arm, "Vaults, that's what we want."

Lucy looked at Druid.

"Vaults," nodded Druid, his eyes gleaming darkly at the thought of gold. The signs reading 'Vaults' led them down more and more steps, deeper and deeper into the ground. Once, in the distance, they thought they heard footsteps, but they faded away. Then the sign changed. Coming down a very narrow flight of steps, the door in front of them read:

'THE VAULTS OF THE BANK OF ENGLAND. NO UNAUTHORISED ENTRY.'

"What a long name," muttered Ben.

On either side of the door, stood narrow steel bars. Druid floated between them. Lucy, with Ben's help, crawled under the bottom grid.

"See," said Ben, "you're better off being small."

Druid looked about to cry again. Lucy jabbed Ben.

"Shut up and look for treasure."

Rows and rows of large metal boxes filled the vaults from floor to ceiling.

"They're like our school lockers," exclaimed Ben.

"Keep looking," ordered Lucy.

They wandered down the enormous avenues with the high metal cabinets on either side. Druid began to look downcast.

"We should open one up to see if there is any gold in it," suggested Ben. Druid stopped and pressed his nostrils against one of the boxes.

"No gold," he sniffed.

"No, but maybe there are some diamonds or pearls in there. They're still treasure, aren't they?" reasoned Lucy.

Druid's eyes lit up. He needed gold, but he ought to have some precious stones as well. Druid considered the box. Then, using his smallest claw, he began to crack the lock. A minute passed. Ben yawned. The box sprang open.

"No lock can a dragon stop," confided Druid.

Ben and Lucy waited. Druid lifted out the box's secret treasure.

"Paper," muttered Lucy with disappointment.

"Tied up with ribbons," observed Ben in disgust.

Druid spluttered fire in distress. The papers fell to ashes on the floor. Lucy took Druid's claw and led him away.

"Keep looking," she urged Ben, "there must be some treasure here somewhere."

"Over here, Luce," came Ben's voice a short while later, "quick, over here."

Lucy ran towards her brother's voice, Druid cruising beside her. Ben was standing in a room lined with shelves stacked high with brown sacks.

"Look," pointed Ben, dragging out one of the sacks and pulling it open. One pound coins cascaded onto the floor. Lucy leapt with delight. Within minutes they had made a mountain of money. Lucy and Ben danced around, sprinkling money everywhere.

"Thousands and thousands," sang Lucy.

"Millions and millions," cried Ben.

"Come on, Druid," shouted Lucy, "sit on top of your treasure."

Druid flew to the top of the pile of money. He sparked with laughter and showered handfuls of coins onto Lucy and Ben as they danced around the money. As he scooped up another clawful, Druid stopped. Picking up a single coin, he squinted at it, sniffed it, bit it in half and spat it out.

"No gold," judged the dragon.

"What?" said Lucy, her arms full of pound coins.

"No gold," repeated Druid, his eyes beginning to fill with tears.

"What a rip-off!" cried Ben, dropping his handfuls of coins.

"Don't cry, Druid," warned Lucy, waving her finger at the small red dragon, "we'll find you a treasure. We'll just have to look somewhere else."

Druid nodded dumbly.

"Yes, we will," agreed Ben, "since it's almost tea time."

Lucy studied her watch. It was a quarter to five.

"Come on," led Lucy, with the dragon following, "let's go home. We'll think of a better place to find Druid a treasure."

Ben stood for a second, then reached out for a small brown bag of coins.

"Ben!"

Ben's arm stopped.

"No gold," reminded Druid.

"But it's a lot of sweets, Druid," Ben said wistfully.

"No gold, no good," stated the dragon firmly.

Ben nodded and followed.

Getting out of the Bank of England was even easier than getting in had been.

"These doors are to stop people getting in, not out," Lucy explained.

None of the passers-by hurrying home along Threadneedle

Street noticed the two small figures and an even smaller red dragon step out of a small side-door of the Bank of England, closing it quietly behind them.

They headed home for tea, leaving thousands of pound coins scattered across the floor and millions of pounds of stocks, shares and deeds burnt to a cinder.

The red-eyed dragon was smuggled some more sandwiches, then put to bed, with Lucy and Ben promising to think of another way of finding the greatest treasure in the world.

CHAPTER
FOUR

Anna, Lucy and Ben's older sister, was sitting at the kitchen table. She was struggling with her homework. Lucy sat down opposite her. Anna kept on working. It was best to ignore little sisters.

"What," asked Lucy casually, "is the greatest treasure in the world?"

"The Crown Jewels," Anna answered shortly.

A thoughtful pause followed.

"Where are the Crown Jewels kept?" Lucy asked, trying to sound calm.

Anna stopped writing.

"In the Tower of London, birdbrain."

There followed an even more thoughtful pause.

"Blast," muttered Anna, reaching for her rubber.

"The Crown Jewels in the Tower of London," beamed Lucy, leaving her sister to rub out her mistake.

"We can't just walk in and ask to open an account there," said Ben.

Druid agreed.

"We don't need to," smiled Lucy with a knowing twinkle.

Ben and Druid waited.

"Where did Miss Brown say we were going on the school trip on Friday?" asked Lucy, mimicking her teacher's voice.

"To see the Beefeaters," remembered Ben, a wide smile growing, "at the Tower of London."

Druid clapped his claws and flapped his wings.

"A tidy idea," chuckled the red dragon, blowing smoke rings in his excitement.

The day of the trip arrived. Druid, with protests, was squashed into Ben's bag. The dragon was smuggled on to the coach. Past the gates, past the Beefeaters and into the Tower.

A Yeoman Warder, as Beefeaters are properly known, led the classes through the courtyard. Lucy and Ben, carrying the bag with Druid inside between them, walked slowly at the back of their classes. The Beefeater, in a deep military voice, was booming out the names of the different parts of the Tower.

"Come along, Lucy, Benjamin," rang out Miss Brown's voice, when she noticed the two of them were lagging behind.

"Coming, Miss," they answered, turning left as the Beefeater led the classes right.

"Quick," whispered Lucy, dropping the bag with a thud, "which way, Druid?"

Druid's legs appeared first. He emerged rubbing his head.

"I'm not made of metal, you know," he moaned.

"Hurry up, Druid," pleaded Lucy, as the dragon made a great show of checking himself for bruises.

"Nothing broken, I'm glad to say," hummed the dragon.

"Come on, Druid," urged Ben, on the look out for Beefeaters.

"Alright, alright," grumbled the dragon, who did not like to be rushed.

Druid took a deep breath and stood to his full height, which was not very tall.

"It's here," hissed Druid, his eyes glinting, "follow me."

Lucy and Ben scrambled to keep up with the treasure-hungry dragon. Through many twists and turns, avoiding patrolling Beefeaters, Druid led them, climbing worn stone steps to an arched wooden door. The door had a large iron keyhole.

"Humph," grunted the dragon, using his largest claw to spring the old lock, "easy-peasy."

Together they pushed open the heavy, oak door. The room was dark and smelled very old. Against the walls stood great wooden chests. Each chest had a strong iron padlock.

"Which one?" asked Ben.

"Sssh," said Lucy.

Druid began to pick one of the padlocks, his teeth chattering with excitement. They pushed the lid of the chest back.

"Jewels," murmured Lucy.

"Silver," gasped Ben.

"Gold!" rasped Druid, throwing gold coins, sovereigns and doubloons, into the air.

Then he fainted.

Druid came round to find himself sitting on a pile of gold coins, goblets, keys and crowns. Lucy and Ben, wearing ill-fitting crowns, were each sitting on smaller mounds of treasure.

"We saved this one for you," said Lucy, placing a crown of gold and jewels on Druid's head.

Now they each had a crown. All the crowns were too big.

"How are we going to get it all home?" asked Lucy, straightening her crown.

They all sat thinking, each upon a heap of treasure.

"In our bag?" suggested Ben.

"We haven't got enough room in our bag," replied Lucy, then an idea formed, "but the rest of our classes will have."

"We can't tell them," protested Ben.

"We'll have to," decided Lucy.

Leaving the dragon to count his new hoard, Lucy and Ben sneaked back to find their classes in the Armoury. It took all their powers of persuasion, to get the first few classmates to come with them, but the chance to meet a real red dragon was too good to miss. Ben introduced his three dumbstruck friends to Druid, now quite comfortable on HIS treasure.

"Salutations," bowed the dragon.

Ben began to give his friends' names.

"No time for formalities now," instructed the dragon, eager to leave with the loot, "pleased to meet you. Quickly, fill up your bags. Be tidy about it."

Ben's friends did exactly as the dragon told them. The word spread quickly through the class. Working in relays, the Jewel Room was soon empty. Druid, like an emperor marching in triumph, refused to go back into Ben's bag.

"If you get seen," warned Lucy.

The dragon waved her objections aside. The coach journey

back was a slow one. Miss Brown, sitting at the front near the driver, was pleased that the classes made no noise the whole way. On the back seat of the coach, the dragon was holding court, giving his version of the tale of St George. No one breathed a word.

"You all know what to do," Lucy reminded them, as the coach began to drop them off near their homes, "and remember, not a word to anyone."

"Sssh!" added Druid.

CHAPTER
FIVE

"How many more people have got to drop off homework with you this evening, Lucy?" asked Lucy's Dad, after the nineteenth or twentieth bag of 'homework' had been delivered by yet another classmate.

"Just a few more, Dad," replied Lucy innocently.

Ben looked at his plate and ate his tea. There was safety in silence. Later that evening, a meeting was held in Ben's room. A sparkling mountain of treasure rested against the bed, Druid at its peak. Coins trickled down to where Lucy and Ben sat on its slopes.

"We have to think of a way for Druid to take the treasure home," explained Lucy.

Druid nodded.

"Why can't you stay here?" Ben asked Druid.

"Because we haven't got room," answered his sister, "especially when Druid begins to grow."

Lucy looked to the dragon for support. Druid nodded sadly.

"It just wouldn't be tidy for me to stay here, Ben," spoke the dragon kindly.

The bedroom door opened and in walked Anna.

"Lucy, have you seen my..." Anna began.

She stared in amazement at the splendid pile of gold. But, most of all, at the magnificent red dragon.

"Hello, Anna, you haven't met Druid, have you?" said Ben.

"Salutations, fair Anna, honoured to meet you," responded the dragon, bowing low.

"Don't scream," ordered Lucy as her sister's mouth twitched.

Holding Anna's hand, Lucy explained how they had met Druid and why the Crown Jewels were there. Anna did not utter a word. She just stared numbly at the dragon and the treasure. Lucy led her elder sister to bed.

The next morning, Anna knocked on the door before entering. Closing the door behind her, she looked at brother, sister and the dragon. The treasure had gone.

"Where has it all gone?" stammered Anna.

"In the toy chest," said Ben.

"Under the bed," answered Lucy.

"In the wardrobes," added her brother.

"Druid flew some up to the loft," explained her sister.

"Everywhere," finished Druid, waving his claws around the room.

"What if Mum finds it?" Anna whispered, leaning against the door as the dragon spoke.

"She won't unless you tell her," charged Lucy.

Three pairs of eyes bore into her.

Anna decided to help them and she had a plan. Her class were going on a biology field trip on Sunday. They were visiting Pembroke in Wales.

"We're taking three full trunks of equipment with us. We could put the treasure inside them instead," explained Anna.

The others agreed. That night, with great stealth, the substitution was made.

"Now, don't forget," said the grateful dragon, trying not to cry as he bid them goodbye, "if you ever need my help, ask the Earthstone at dawn or dusk. I'm always in then."

Druid shook hands and bowed to them all. In a most un-dragon like gesture, Druid gave them a big bag of gold coins to share with all the classmates who had helped them.

The whole family came to wave goodbye to Anna. Druid was sneaked on to the coach in Anna's bag, his head sticking out of the top. It took the driver, the teacher and four dads to lift each of the trunks onto the coach.

The journey was a slow one. The coach crawled along the road, its secret cargo weighing it down.

Druid and Anna sat near the back, although she insisted that the small dragon stay in her bag. Anna was worried that at any moment the Crown Jewels would be mentioned on the coach's radio. Very late that afternoon, the coach finally arrived at the large old house, where the class would be staying. Anna watched as the very heavy trunks were unloaded and left in the wide hallway. Anna unpacked slowly and as soon as her roommates had gone downstairs, she let Druid out. The dragon strutted along the windowsill.

"What wonderful Welsh air," breathed Druid deeply, "very tidy, but I wish Lucy and Ben were here."

In the morning, the hallway was empty. The trunks had vanished. So had Druid.

The biology teacher, Mr. Green, was very upset and called the police. Anna tried to forget about the dragon and the jewels. But she was not allowed to. Late that afternoon, Mr. Green summoned her to his office, where a police officer was waiting to speak to her.

"It appears, Anna," began Mr. Green, nervously, "that your brother and sister are in serious trouble."

Mr. Green paused and the police officer continued.

"The Crown Jewels have been stolen from the Tower of London. We have reason to believe that members of your brother's and sister's school may have had something to do with it."

"The entire school, including all the teachers, has been arrested," spluttered Mr. Green.

"It would appear that all the members of two particular classes each have a gold coin taken from the Crown Jewels and that another, er um," the policeman did not want to use the word 'dragon', "being may be involved."

"That silly, Druid," thought Anna, "giving everybody a gold coin before he left."

Mr. Green cleared his throat.

"I'm afraid that you and Emily, who also has a brother in that class, will have to go back to London immediately."

"Have you anything to say, Anna?" Mr. Green asked quietly, his voice shaking slightly.

"Can I go to the toilet, please?" Anna asked, her mind racing ahead.

Mr. Green nodded.

"I must find Druid and bring the Crown Jewels back," decided Anna as she pulled on her coat.

Anna ran:

Away from the house.

Over the fields.

Into the hills.

On and on.

Darkness closed in around her, but she kept going. Gradually, weariness began to catch up with her. She stumbled on.

Anna awoke feeling very cold. The sun was just peeping over the horizon. She had fallen asleep against one of a ring of tall standing stones.

"Oh, Druid, please help us!" she cried, pressing against the old smooth stone.

The sun light struck the stone.

"Salutations, fair Anna," Druid sat on the flat rock behind her.

Anna, her voice rising in panic, explained what had happened to Lucy and Ben. Druid sat in silence.

"You must give the Crown Jewels back," begged Anna.

"Return my treasure?" Cried the red dragon fiercely.

"But it's not yours, you stole it," persisted the girl.

Druid looked at his feet.

"If I return my treasure I shall never grow," mused the small red dragon. "No dragon has ever willingly given up a treasure."

They sat together as the full rays of the sun struck Druid.

"I have grown a little since yesterday, haven't I?" Druid asked quietly.

Anna did not answer.

"But," decided the fine red dragon, "I have missed Lucy and Ben more than I have grown."

However, Druid refused to give the treasure to the police.

"If it is to be returned, it must be to the person who had it before I did," announced the dragon, careful not to use the word 'stolen'.

That evening, a small, heavily weighed-down, minibus, driven by a very nervous Mr. Green, turned into Pall Mall. Beside him on the front seat sat Anna and Druid. Druid was explaining at great length, the history of dragons. Over the radio, they had learnt that Lucy and Ben were being sent to the Tower of London. Members of Parliament were calling for charges of treason.

The police officer on duty at the gates was too shocked to refuse the dragon's request. The minibus, bearing a red dragon, two people and, of course, the Crown Jewels, stopped inside the inner courtyard of Buckingham Palace.

Flying up to the nearest Coldstream Guard, Druid requested an audience with the Queen. The soldier took one look at the bright red dragon and dashed off to fetch his sergeant. The sergeant, upon seeing the hovering dragon, trotted off to get the Officer of the Guard. Druid and Anna stood waiting. Mr. Green had to sit down as his legs were shaking too much.

They were surrounded by the entire Palace Guard.

"Not as tidy a colour as my coat," remarked Druid, looking at the soldiers' bold red jackets.

After all, he was a dragon and vanity is a particular trait in dragons. Finally, the Queen's Private Secretary arrived.

"Sir Crispin Pemberton Ottley-Smythe," began the tall stately gentleman.

Druid bowed and gave his full name, as he did to all knights. This took quite a while, as his proper name was very long.

"Where's your steed?" demanded Druid.

The knight was very startled and mumbled something about protocol. The dragon bowed very low.

"I request an audience with Her Majesty, The Queen."

Sir Crispin regretted that an audience was out of the question. Druid frowned and then did what dragons have done for thousands of years. He set fire to the man's moustache. The Private Secretary scuttled away, without his moustache.

A few minutes later, Druid was guided through the Palace. Anna was left to wait with a trembling Mr. Green. Druid was led into a magnificent audience room.

"Her Majesty, The Queen," announced Sir Crispin, his stiff, upper lip still smarting.

The doors closed behind Druid.

CHAPTER
SIX

Anna thought she was dreaming. She was driven home in a royal Rolls Royce. Lucy and Ben, with their parents, were waiting for her. As Anna stepped out of the car, the driver handed her a letter. In the house, the whole family sat still as Anna opened it.

"It's from The Queen," gasped Anna, scanning the lines ahead.

"Well, read it then, birdbrain," said Ben impatiently.

"It says the Crown Jewels have been returned safely and that no great harm has been done," Anna looked up with relief.

Lucy and Ben were relieved as well.

"What about Druid?" demanded Ben.

"Druid has been sent to the Tower of London," said Anna.

"Oh, no," wailed Ben.

"They can't do that," protested Lucy.

Anna looked at them, then began to read again.

"I hereby appoint," Anna paused, "what a long name he's got!"

"I hereby appoint Druid as the Keeper of the Crown Jewels for as long as he so wishes. Signed The Queen."

"Hurray!" cheered Lucy.

The whole family danced with joy.

"Just think," said Ben to his sisters, "we'll be able to visit him every day."

Ben, Lucy and Anna did see Druid again, although not quite every day as Ben had predicted. It was after one such visit that Ben raised a subject that had been bothering him for some time.

"I thought that gold was supposed to make dragons bigger?" questioned Ben.

"It is," answered Anna.

"Then, why isn't Druid getting any bigger? He spends all his time sitting on the greatest treasure in the world, and he's still a squirt," said Ben.

"Don't be so rude, Ben," said his eldest sister.

"But he is," protested Ben.

"Druid will never grow," said Lucy.

The other two stared at her.

"What?" exclaimed Ben and Anna.

"It isn't gold that makes dragons grow," Lucy informed them.

"What is it then?" demanded her brother, annoyed that Lucy might really know and he did not.

"It is the love of gold that makes them grow," continued Lucy, who had obviously given the matter a lot of thought, "and Druid doesn't love gold, he loves us."

Lucy smiled.

Anna and Ben looked at each other. They walked on a few paces along by the Thames.

"Is it the same with us?" Ben asked finally.

They both waited for Lucy's answer.

Lucy smiled, shook her head and smiled again.

She did not know.

Special thanks to

ZEE

and

Denise, Joanne, Katie, Lynne & Presch

* * *